USBORNE BIBLE TALES

Jonah and the Whale

Retold by Heather Amery
Designed by Maria Wheatley
Illustrated by Norman Young

Language consultant: Betty Root
Series editor: Jenny Tyler

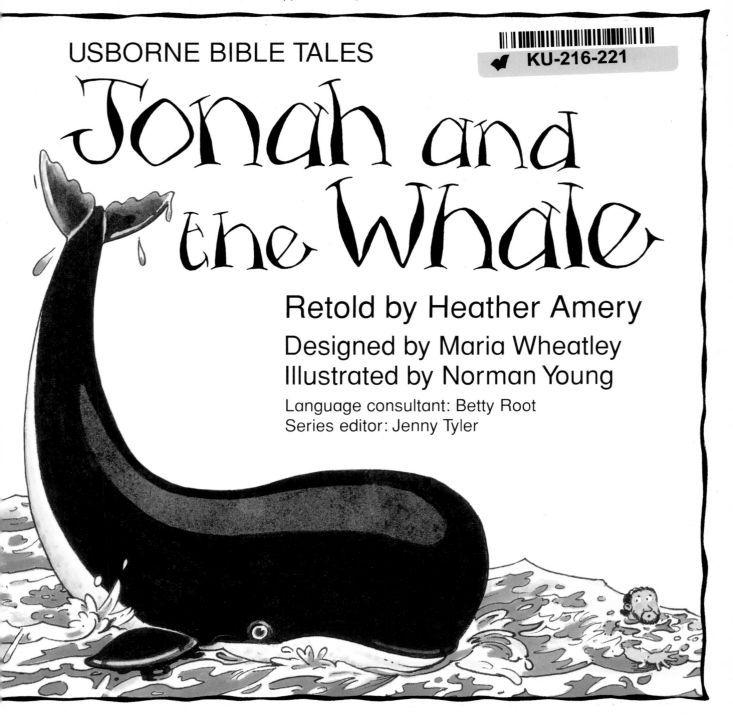

This is Jonah.

He lived a very long time ago in a country called Israel. He was a good man who believed in God.

"Go to Nineveh," said God.

"The people there are very wicked. Tell them to be good and obey me."

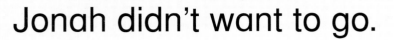

Jonah didn't want to go.

"I'll go to Tarshish," he thought. "God won't be able
to see me there." And he set off.

At the port he got on a ship.

Jonah paid his fare and the ship left for Tarshish.
But soon there was a terrible storm.

The sailors were terrified.

They prayed to their gods to save them but the storm got worse. Jonah slept through it all.

The captain woke Jonah.

"Ask your God to save us," he said. Jonah was
trying to hide from God so he wouldn't pray.

"Throw me into the sea."

"That will save you," said Jonah. "I can't," said the captain. But some men grabbed Jonah.

They threw Jonah overboard.

Just at that moment, the storm stopped. The sailors thanked Jonah's God for saving them.

Jonah sank down into the sea.

"I am going to drown," thought Jonah. Suddenly a huge whale swam up and swallowed Jonah whole.

" God has saved me."

"I'm still alive," thought Jonah. "It's very dark and wet inside this whale."

Jonah lived in the whale for three days.

Then the whale swam to a beach. It opened its mouth and spat Jonah out onto dry land.

"Go to Nineveh," said God.

"All right, God. I'll go now," said Jonah and he walked all the way to the great city.

"You must stop being wicked," said Jonah.

"Or God will destroy your city." The King told the people that they must obey God.

Jonah sat outside the city.

He waited for it to be destroyed. But God saw that the people had changed and spared the city.

"I love all the people, Jonah."

"And I am everywhere," said God. "You can't run away from me." Jonah knew this was true.

First published in 1996 by Usborne Publishing Ltd, 83-85 Saffron Hill, London EC1N 8RT, England. Copyright © Usborne Publishing Ltd. The name Usborne and the device are Trade Marks of Usborne Publishing Ltd. All rights reserved. No part of this publication may be reproduced, stored in a retrieval system, or transmitted in any form or by any means, electronic, mechanical, photocopy, recording or otherwise, without prior permission of the publisher. UE First published in America in March 1997. Printed in Belgium.

THIS BLOOMSBURY BOOK

BELONGS TO

....

On My Way to the Bath

Sarah Maizes

Illustrated by
Michael Paraskevas

BLOOMSBURY

LONDON BERLIN NEW YORK SYDNEY

Bloomsbury Publishing, London, Berlin, New York and Sydney

First published in Great Britain in May 2012 by Bloomsbury Publishing Plc
50 Bedford Square, London, WC1B 3DP

A CIP catalogue record for this book is available from the British Library

ISBN 978 1 4088 2588 4

Printed in China by C & C Offset Printing Co Ltd, Shenzhen, Guangdong

1 3 5 7 9 10 8 6 4 2

Book design by Donna Mark

www.bloomsbury.com

MIX
Paper from
responsible sources
FSC
www.fsc.org   FSC® C008047

For Izzy, Ben and, of course, Livi
S.M.

As always for my wonderful mother, Betty
M.P.

I do not want to have a bath. Baths are boring. Everything is more fun than baths.

On my way to the bath, I slither off the sofa. I am a snake. I slink, I slide. I stick my tongue out at my brother.

On my way to the bath, I see my blocks
on the sitting room floor. I will make a statue.
It will be a statue of me. Holding a cat.

On my way to the bath, I do a cartwheel. I am a professional gymnastics girl. I bend, I balance and stretch... Watch me do a perfect split...

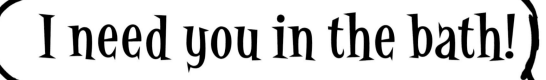

On my way to the bath, I see my sister in her room – she's listening to music. Hey, I can sing that song! JUST like a rock star...
'LA, LA, LA, LAAAAAAAA!!!!!!'
I will put on a show!

On my way to the bath, I pass the guinea pigs, Leo and Melly, my loyal minions. It's time to plan our latest caper. They will help me rule the world!

On my way to the bath, I march. I am in a parade! I play the tuba. As I march down the street, the crowd goes wild for my tuba solo! BWWWWWAAAAAHHHHHHH!

On my way to the bath, I pass through a jungle. A thick, dark jungle. I am looking for sloths. Oh no! Quicksand! I swing to safety!

On my way to the bath, I hide
behind the bathroom door.
I am a jungle cat . . .
I see an unsuspecting
hedgehog . . .

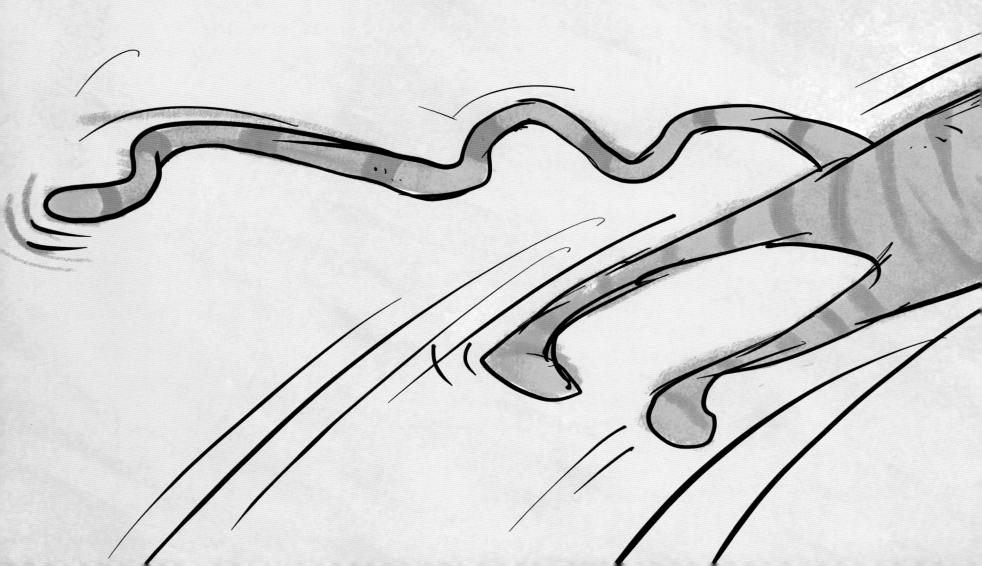

I play. I use soap. I use my sea horse flannel to get very, very clean. Even my toes are clean. Toes are my sea horse's speciality.

I am a shark . . .